TiFFanY DiNO WORKS OUT

Written by Marjorie Weinman Sharmat

Illustrated by Nate Evans

Simon & Schuster Books for Young Readers

SIMON & SCHUSTER BOOKS FOR YOUNG READERS
An imprint of Simon & Schuster Children's Publishing Division
1230 Avenue of the Americas, New York, New York 10020

SIMON & SCHUSTER BOOKS FOR YOUNG READERS
is a trademark of Simon & Schuster.

The text for this book is set in Clearface.
The illustrations are rendered in a mixture of acrylics and gouache.
Manufactured in the United States of America
First edition
10 9 8 7 6 5 4 3 2 1

LIBRARY OF CONGRESS CATALOGING-IN-PUBLICATION DATA

Sharmat, Marjorie Weinman.
Tiffany Dino works out / by Marjorie Weinman Sharmat ;
illustrated by Nate Evans. — 1st ed.
p.   cm.
Summary: Unhappy with her size, Tiffany Dino tries a variety
of activities with her friends in order to lose weight.
ISBN 0-689-80309-5
[1. Dinosaurs—Fiction. 2. Size—Fiction. 3. Exercise—Fiction.
4. Friendship—Fiction.] I. Evans, Nate, ill. II. Title.
PZ7.S5299Ti   1995   94-32995
[E]—dc20

Dedication:

For Mitch, with thanks for being the
coming-up-with-a-great-idea champ
—M. W. S.

For Mark Stephens and Rich LaPierre,
who are both, in their own unique ways,
wonderful artists and inspiring teachers
—N. E.

Tiffany Dinosaur bought a bus. Then she got in it and drove to the supermarket to do her weekly shopping. Tiffany bought

    30 pizzas,
    25 quarts of milk,
    14 jars of peanut butter,
    21 loaves of bread,
    43 boxes of cookies,
    18 bananas,
    15 pounds of nuts,
and 10 bunches of grapes.

"I hope this is enough for the week," she said. Then Tiffany drove home.

On her way, she passed her friend Flexall Dino. He was jogging. "Such energy!" thought Tiffany.

Then she passed Philippe Dino, who was dancing on his toes. "Such zest!" thought Tiffany.

Then she passed Arabella Dino, who was doing cartwheels. "Such zip!" thought Tiffany. Tiffany waved to her friends.

When she got home, she took some bags of groceries from the bus and started to walk through her doorway. "Ouch!" she cried. Tiffany was stuck in the doorway.

"Well, I am certainly stupid, trying to get so
many bags of groceries through my doorway at the
same time," she said.

Tiffany put down half the bags. "Now!" she said,
trying again. "Ouch! What is going on here?"
thought Tiffany. "My doorway must have shrunk."

Tiffany dropped her groceries. Then she
squeezed through the doorway. "Ouch again!"

She looked at herself in her mirror. "Tiffany Dino, you have gotten big," she said.

She stepped on her scale. "Six hundred and fifteen pounds!" she cried. "I have *gained* fifteen pounds! I must *lose* fifteen pounds. No more snacking for Tiffany Dino. I will just sit down and think of thin things."

Tiffany sat down. The chair squeaked. The chair sagged. "Noisy chair. It makes me hungry to listen to it!"

Tiffany went outside and finished unloading her bus. Then she grabbed some food. "A feast! A feast!" shouted Tiffany as she ate and ate.

She looked in her mirror. "Now I am so big I cannot see all of me." Tiffany stepped on her scale. "Six hundred and nineteen pounds!" she exclaimed. "What have I done?" Tiffany went to her telephone. "I hope my friends are home now."

Tiffany telephoned Flexall. "Flexall, I am huge," she said.

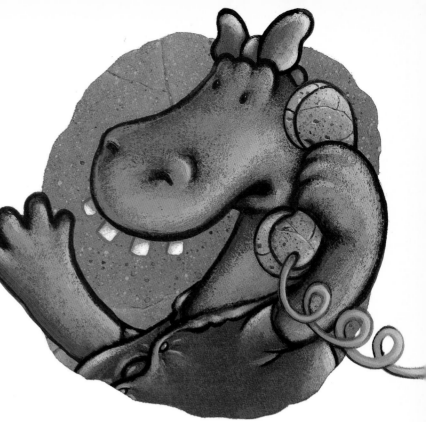

"Me, too," said Flexall. "Isn't it nice?"

"No, I am not *plain* huge," said Tiffany. "I am *hugely* huge, Flexall. I need some help."

Tiffany telephoned Philippe and Arabella. "Your big friend needs help," she said. Tiffany's friends rushed over.

"Sit," said Tiffany. Everyone sat. "How much do you weigh?" Tiffany asked everyone.

"Five hundred and eighty-four pounds," said Arabella.

"Four hundred and ninety-eight," said Philippe.

"Five hundred and two," said Flexall.

"I knew it! I knew it!" cried Tiffany. "Everyone is thin except me."

"But you're a perfect friend," said Philippe.

"Really tops," said Arabella.

"It makes me feel good just to be with you," said Flexall.

Then everyone tried to hug Tiffany. "Oh dear," said Tiffany. "I am so big you can't even reach all the way around me. What can I do?"

"Well, I jog every day," said Flexall.

"I dance," said Philippe.

"I do cartwheels and push-ups," said Arabella.

"Maybe I will try those things," said Tiffany. The next day Tiffany put on her shorts. "These are so tight they will rip if I breathe the wrong way," she thought.

Then she went out jogging with Flexall. "Sometimes I jog in place," said Flexall. "Sometimes I jog backward. I try to make it interesting."

Tiffany and Flexall ran all over town. Tiffany huffed and puffed. When she got home she stepped on the scale.

"Six hundred and eighteen and one-half pounds. I lost only half a pound," she said.

Tiffany called Philippe. "I want to dance," she said.

"Okay," said Philippe. Tiffany put on some yellow tights. It was hard to do.

"If I kick the wrong way, they will surely split," thought Tiffany. Tiffany and Philippe went to dancing class.

"I try to do something each day for my toes,"
said Philippe. "When my toes feel good, I feel good."
Philippe danced on his toes.

"My toes like to be left alone," said Tiffany. But
she kicked and bent and swirled and twirled.

When she got home, she stepped on her scale. "Six hundred and eighteen pounds and one quarter," she said. "I lost only a quarter of a pound."

Tiffany called Arabella. "I am ready for cartwheels and push-ups," she said. Tiffany put on her gym suit. "If I bulge much more, I will bulge right through this suit," she thought.

Tiffany and Arabella went to the gym. "I'm the cartwheel champ," said Arabella as she flipped around the room. "There is something about being upside down that makes me feel so right side up."

Tiffany hung from bars and jumped through hoops. "I'd like to be the sitting-down-and-doing-nothing champ," she thought.

When Tiffany got home, she weighed herself.
"Six hundred and eighteen pounds and one quarter.
I did not lose anything!" she cried.

Tiffany looked in the mirror. "I am one huge
hunk of dinosaur meat. That is what I am."

The next day Tiffany went jogging with Flexall. "Isn't it a nice, crisp day," said Flexall.

"Why don't you spread a little mustard on me," muttered Tiffany.

She went dancing with Philippe. "I learned a new step," said Philippe.

"Maybe add a pickle," muttered Tiffany.

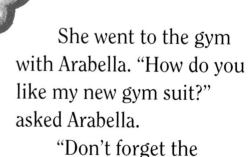

She went to the gym with Arabella. "How do you like my new gym suit?" asked Arabella.

"Don't forget the tomato and lettuce," said Tiffany.

Tiffany went home. "Why should I care about nice, crisp days and new dance steps and new gym suits when I am the biggest dinosaur on the block?"

Tiffany phoned Flexall. "This is gigantic Tiffany," she said. "Please come over."

Tiffany called Philippe. "This is Tiffany, who weighs only slightly less than six hundred and nineteen pounds. Please come over."

Tiffany called Arabella. "This is Tiffany the Huge. Please come over."

Everybody came over. They all tried to hug Tiffany. "I am not huggable!" cried Tiffany. And she ran to her room.

Flexall, Philippe, and Arabella called, "Come back, Tiffany!"

But Tiffany did not come back.

"Tiffany," Flexall called out. "Big, small, any way at all, we like you."

"You're our friend," said Philippe.

"Any size, any shape," said Arabella.

Tiffany didn't answer. At last her friends went home.

Tiffany went to bed. She tossed and turned.

Suddenly she sat up.

"I know what is wrong with me!" she cried. "It is not my big *body*. It is my small *brain*. All I talk about is how big I am. I am lucky I did not lose my friends."

Tiffany wrote herself a note:

The next day Tiffany sold her bus. "Now I will only eat what I can carry home from the supermarket!" Every day, for the next two weeks, Tiffany went out early in the morning. First she put on her shorts and jogged along with Flexall. Tiffany talked about flowers, the weather, stockings, and lampposts.

Then Tiffany put on her tights and went to dancing class. She talked about dance steps, telephones, trees, and photographs while she danced with Philippe.

Then Tiffany put on her gym suit and went to the gym. She talked about letters, the color green, gym suits, and robins while she and Arabella did push-ups.

One day Flexall said, "You're fun, Tiffany."

"And very good company," added Philippe.

"And a great push-ups partner," said Arabella.

Tiffany felt happy. She ran home and dashed through her doorway. She did not bump against either side of it. "That is strange," thought Tiffany.

She sat down in her chair. It did not squeak. It did not sag. "No squeaks, no sags. All *very* strange," thought Tiffany.

Tiffany got up and went to her scale. She weighed herself. "Six hundred and thirteen pounds! Tiffany Dino is getting small!"

Then Tiffany heard a
noise. "That is not a squeak,"
she said. "That's a roar."

Tiffany looked out her
window. She saw a moving
truck next door.

"I am getting a new
neighbor," she thought. "I
will take over some flowers
and say hello."

Tiffany went next door
with her flowers. "Yoo-hoo!
Welcome!" she called.
Suddenly a huge dinosaur
appeared.

"Hi, I'm Muffy," the
dinosaur said.

Tiffany stared at Muffy. She looked at her, up and down and down and up. She circled her. "You're gorgeous!" said Tiffany. "You're big and beautiful. May I ask how much you weigh?"

"Just a tad over one thousand pounds," Muffy said proudly.

"Nuts! I'm only six hundred and thirteen pounds," said Tiffany. "I'm too skinny. I knew it! I knew it!"

"So what?" said Muffy. "Big or small, you seem like an okay dinosaur to me."

"Really? That's what all my friends tell me," said Tiffany. Tiffany scratched her head. "Hmm. I feel like an okay dino."

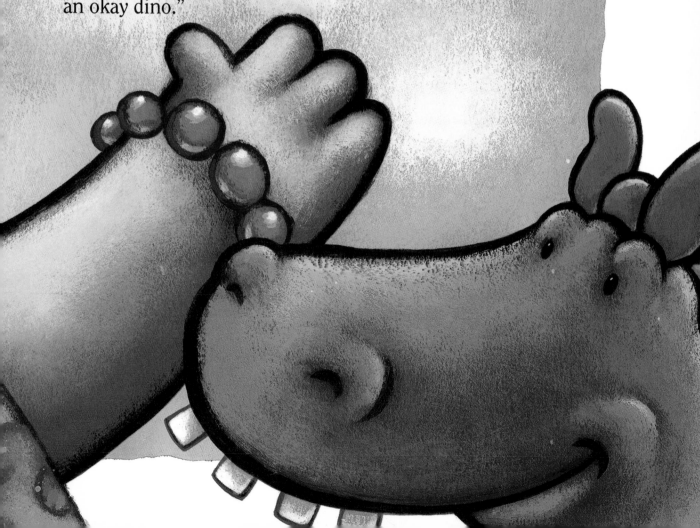

Tiffany gave Muffy a welcome hug. She couldn't reach all the way around her. Then they went into Muffy's house and unpacked her furniture.

J F S531t

Sharmat, Marjorie Weinman.

Tiffany Dino works out

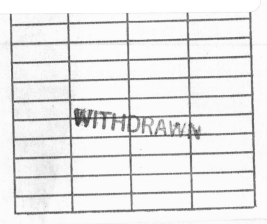

Cressman Library
Cedar Crest College
Allentown, Pa. 18104

DEMCO